KIT KITTEN AND THE TOPSY-TURVY FEELINGS

A Story About Parents Who Aren't Always Able to Care

Jane Evans

Illustrated by Izzy Bean

Jessica Kingsley *Publishers*
London and Philadelphia

First published in 2015
by Jessica Kingsley Publishers
73 Collier Street
London N1 9BE, UK
and
400 Market Street, Suite 400
Philadelphia, PA 19106, USA

www.jkp.com

Library of Congress Cataloging in Publication Data
Evans, Jane, 1961-
Kit Kitten and the topsy turvy feelings : learning about parents who aren't always able to care / Jane Evans.
pages cm
ISBN 978-1-84905-602-1 (alk. paper)
1. Emotions--Juvenile literature. 2. Emotions in children--Juvenile literature. 3. Parent and child--Juvenile literature. 4. Parents--Mental health--Juvenile literature. I. Title.
BF723.E6E93 2015
152.4--dc23
2015000548

British Library Cataloguing in Publication Data
A CIP catalogue record for this book is available from the British Library

ISBN 978 1 84905 602 1
eISBN 978 1 78450 064 1

Printed and bound in China

Dear Child,

I wrote this story about Kit Kitten for you because, just like Kit, you are growing up and knowing more every day. Being able to work out what the feelings are in your body, and having names for them, can be useful for learning more about yourself. Being able to understand other people's feelings, so you can tell when they need someone to play with or for someone to ask whether they are OK, can be good for you, and for them too.

Everyone is full of feelings. If you can begin to get to know yours and feel able to tell others what they are, it will help to keep you safe and well. It can then give them a chance to listen and to help you if you are worried or sad about something.

In this story, once Kit can talk about feelings with the grown-up cats, there is more time to play, learn and have fun (before that, too many feelings are getting in the way!). I hope that Kit's story can help make it easier for you to feel able to tell someone how you are feeling, and that they can learn from Kindly Cat the best way to ask you how you are feeling!

Love from,
Jane

Once upon a time there was a little kitten called Kit Kitten and a big cat called Kizz Cat. They lived together in a flat in a busy town called Kitterly.

Kit Kitten mostly played alone – dashing in and out of the shadows, chasing flies and dancing with sunbeams. This filled Kit Kitten's tummy with warm, cosy feelings.

What do you think these feelings could be?

excited happy

curious

something else

Kit Kitten was growing up and knowing more and more every day.

Kit Kitten knew that rain makes fur wet and cold, that birds are hard to catch, that fences are easy to tumble off, and that tummies with no food in them make noises and sometimes hurt.

What Kit Kitten did not know was how to talk about feelings. Neither the big, medium-sized or small feelings Kit felt inside, nor the feelings Kit saw on the faces of other cats and kittens.

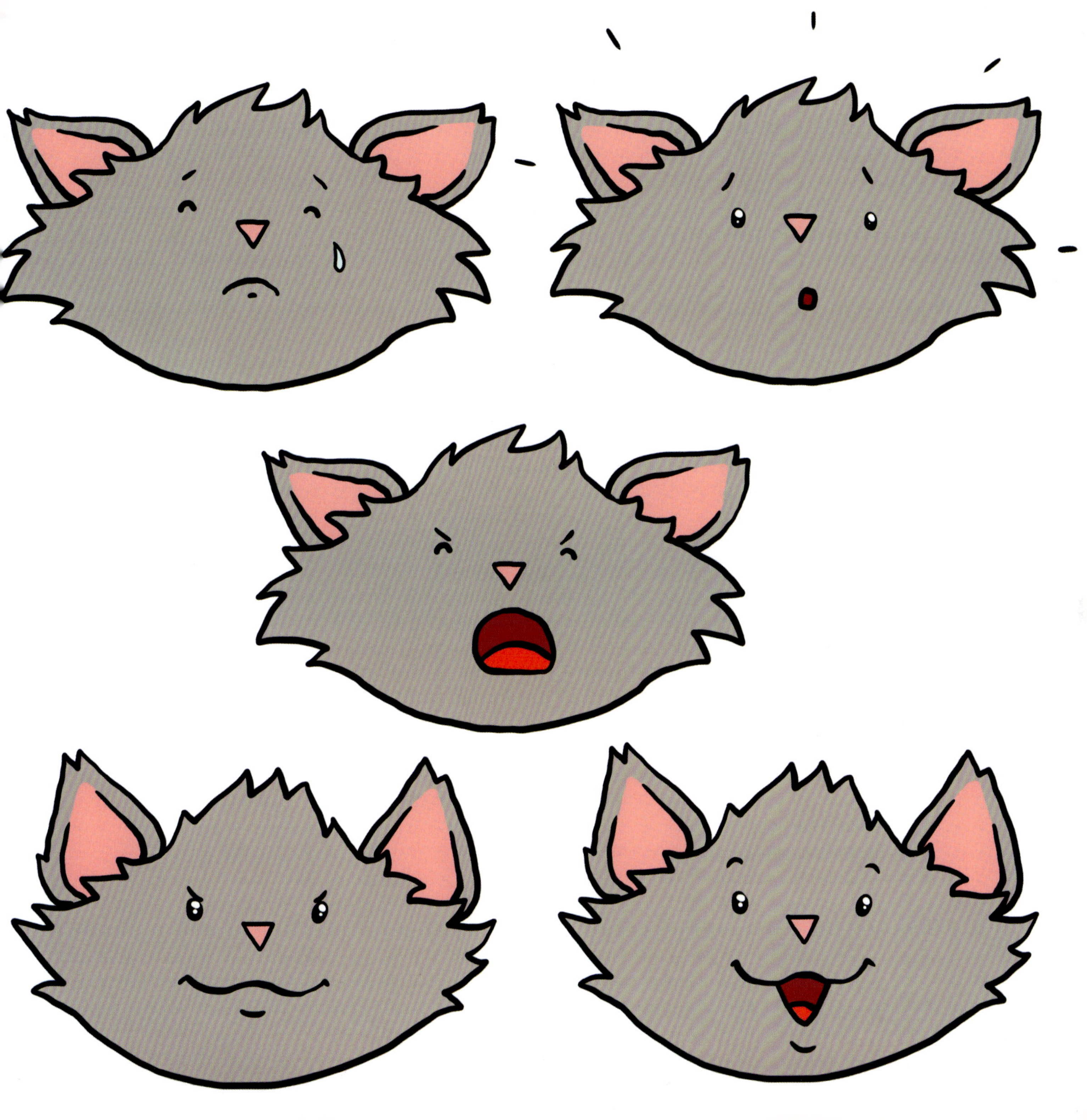

Often Kizz Cat seemed to forget to talk about feelings with Kit, or to ask how Kit was feeling. When Kit's teacher Mr Whiskers did, it was only to say, 'Kit, what's up with you today? You look worried,' or 'You look much happier today, Kit.' All of this was difficult for Kit, because what others said about Kit's feelings didn't always match what Kit felt inside.

Some days, on the walk to school with Kizz Cat, Kit could feel that something was not right. There was no smiling, no talking and no paw-holding. Kit Kitten would go into the classroom full of muddled and mixed up feelings, which made being able to play, learn or make friends hard to do.

OW

Every morning Mr Whiskers patted Kit's head and said, 'Good morning, Kit Kitten! I hope you are ready for a big learning day today?' Kit liked this, but wondered if today would be the day that Mr Whiskers would get upset and shout at everyone; Kit knew this was what big cats often did. So Kit kept still and quiet in class, watching and waiting for this to happen.

What feelings did Kit Kitten have in the classroom every day?

worried scared

lonely

something else

At the end of the school day, Kit had even more feelings, because sometimes Kizz Cat would not be there to collect Kit. When Kizz Cat finally did arrive, there would be no 'Hello Kit, how was your day?' Kizz Cat would walk Kit Kitten home in a wobbly way, often dragging Kit down the road, to a cold flat and no dinner.

On other days, Kizz Cat would be waiting for Kit Kitten in the playground, shouting and laughing loudly, and would rush Kit off to the Fish Shop, saying, 'Have all the fish you want Kit, have them all!'

One morning, Kit Kitten could not get Kizz Cat to wake up in time to go to school. The night before, Kizz Cat had kept them both up late, singing and dancing, and telling jokes and long, long stories.

Kit tried whispering in Kizz's ear, stroking a paw, coughing loudly and then shouting, 'WAKE UP!' But nothing worked, Kizz just snored and rolled over. The flat felt cold, there was no breakfast and Kit did not go to school that day.

How do you think this made Kit feel?

scared anxious

confused

something else

Z Z Z Z

Much later that day there was a knock, knock, knock at the front door. Very slowly, Kizz Cat got up and opened the door. Mr Whiskers was there with Kindly Cat. They came inside and Mr Whiskers said that everyone needs help sometimes, and that was why Kindly Cat had come to see them both.

From that day on, Kindly Cat visited every week and played games and shared books with Kit Kitten and Kizz Cat. Together they learned ways of understanding and talking about feelings – the big, medium-sized and small feelings they felt inside, and the feelings they saw on the faces of other cats and kittens.

Mr Whiskers and Kizz Cat learned that they needed to ask how Kit was feeling, and then wait and wonder a bit at first, to give Kit time to find the words to say, 'I feel calm and happy, thanks!' or 'I am a bit tired and worried today.'

Soon Kit knew that the word for the grey, rainy inside feelings, which are felt when things are not going well (and sometimes tears tumble out), was sad. If Kit could not understand something and had tight, uncomfortable shoulders, that usually meant Kit was a bit worried. When Kit had a chest full of fizzy, whizzy little fireworks, Kit could say, 'I feel SO excited!'

The more Kit started to find names for feelings, the more time there was for playing, learning and making friends. Kizz Cat seemed happier, too, and now their walks home from school were a time to talk about things and look forward to dinner time together.

How about you? What words do you have for your inside feelings? Can you use the Kit Kitten pictures below to work out where you feel them in your body?

Grown-ups' Guide to Using the Storybook

During their early development, children need time with adults who regularly explore, name and wonder about feelings, to develop their ability to process, name and recognise feelings. This enables children to be able to express themselves, which leaves them feeling more relaxed so they are free to explore and learn about the world as a foundation for their development.

A child's mental and physical well-being comes from feeling emotionally comfortable and well-regulated. This they learn from their daily interactions with caring adults, which develop their abilities to work out and put into words their emotions so that eventually they are able to recognise when they feel anxious, excited, scared or sad, and ask for support. This has great benefits for dealing with life's everyday stresses and for building relationships with others.

Kit Kitten lives in a home with an adult carer who has complex needs and struggles to find the words for their own feelings and to tune into Kit's. This may be due to the carer's mental illness, own childhood trauma, substance dependency or domestic abuse. Some days they are depressed and sad, others over-the-top with excitement and enthusiasm. The uncertainty of all of this is especially difficult for Kit, who is not helped to understand feelings or to develop an emotional vocabulary.

Activities

Doing activities with children can be a relaxed way to continue learning about feelings with them. This needs to be done at their pace and attuned to their emotional state. Some children will be wary or uncomfortable, as they may be used to wanting their feelings to be acknowledged but repeatedly being disappointed. Ensure you do the activities in a quiet place, when they are not tired, hungry, hot or thirsty!

If they are reluctant or anxious, use a soft toy kitten or other animal and do the activities with the toy near to the child, or with the child talking about the animal's feelings rather than their own. It may take time and repetition for them to feel comfortable, but it's important to keep trying, and at their pace.

- Use the picture of Kit Kitten and the feelings faces and feelings in the body from page 28 to talk to children about their feelings throughout the day. Gently explore with them how they may be feeling. Do not worry if they don't say much at first; just keep wondering and waiting, without rushing in and telling them, 'I think Kit is feeling…' Try saying, 'I was wondering if…?' or 'If it was me I think I might feel…'

- Using some coloured dot stickers, ask children to decide what colour a certain feeling might be and where it could be felt in their body. Encourage them to put the sticker on the place where they feel it in their bodies; you do the same too. Use this as a fun way to introduce the idea that everyone can experience feelings in different ways. Take a photo of you covered in stickers so you can talk about it at other times as a reminder, or to reflect on changes.

- Draw feelings faces on some strips of coloured card with a child (words too if that helps), then make a small hole in each one and tie them together with some string. Now you have something to pop in your pocket to use to talk about feelings everywhere and anywhere!

- In small groups, throw or pass around a soft toy, making sure each child gets a turn. Simply wonder, 'How is the animal feeling today?' If they struggle, make gentle suggestions based on what feelings you have seen the child present. Explore what the animal might need to feel a bit better.